Far Apart, Close in Heart

Being a Family When a Loved One Is Incarcerated

BECKY BIRTHA

pictures by
MAJA KASTELIC

Albert Whitman & Company
Chicago, Illinois

For Justin, Jayden, and Natalie—BB
To N and L—MK

Library of Congress Cataloging-in-Publication data
is on file with the publisher.

Text copyright © 2017 by Becky Birtha
Pictures copyright © 2017 by Albert Whitman & Company
Pictures by Maja Kastelic
Published in 2017 by Albert Whitman & Company
ISBN 978-0-8075-1275-3
Printed in China
10 9 8 7 6 5 4 3 2 1 LP 20 19 18 17 16
Design by Jordan Kost

For more information about Albert Whitman & Company,
visit our website at www.albertwhitman.com.

Children and parents can't always live together. Parents may have to go away and sometimes stay away for a long time. That's what happens when a parent goes to jail or prison. Lots of children have a parent behind bars.

When your mom or dad goes to jail, you can have all
kinds of feelings. You may have different feelings at the
same time, or one big feeling may push all the others away.

Lacey feels OK in the daytime when she can play with her friends but lonely and scared at night when she's by herself in her room.

Rashid is angry with his mom. The last time she got out of jail, she promised him she was home to stay. Then she broke another law and had to go back to jail.

Juana feels torn apart. Her papi is already in prison
when her mami gets arrested. Juana and her siblings go to
live in different homes because nobody can take them all.
Saying so many good-byes hurts.

If your dad or mom is in prison, you probably have questions. Simple questions can have easy answers, but other questions are harder to answer and may even be hard to ask.

Yen has questions that she doesn't want to ask anyone but her mother. Her father gives her paper and a pencil. Yen writes:

Why are you there?

Is it my fault?

When are you coming home?

Do you still love me?

They mail the letter to her mother.

When other kids hear about Rafael's papa, *they* ask questions.

"What did he do?"

"How many years did he get?"

Rafael feels embarrassed that he doesn't know the answers.

If you don't know how to answer, you can find different ways to respond.

Rafael says, "I don't want to talk about it."

When you have a parent in prison or jail, sometimes friends act differently.

The boys on Jermaine's team call him names. Jermaine is glad their coach puts a stop to that really fast.

Emily's friend Tina won't play with her anymore. Tina says her mother told her to stay away from Emily. Hearing those words might leave you sad, shocked, hurt, or with other feelings.

Emily's friend Josanna says, "Don't worry, Emily.
I will always be your friend." Emily feels grateful to
have a friend like Josanna.

Sometimes if your parent is in jail, *you* act differently.

After his father is gone, Atian starts acting up in class. He was always proud of following school rules, but now he's in trouble all the time. He even fights with his best friend.

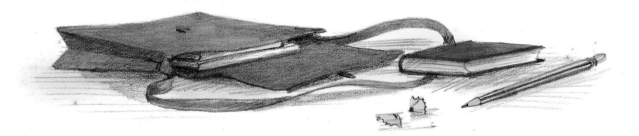

Xavier's dad is in the state penitentiary. "Don't tell anybody!" his mother says. So Xavier doesn't speak at all.

He used to share stories and jokes that his dad told him.
Now he's scared he might tell the secret.

Even when you think nothing can ever get better, things can change. And sometimes you can help make changes. One way is telling someone how you feel.

Juana tells her foster mother how upset she feels with her family scattered all over. Her foster mother lets Juana call each of her siblings.

Atian tells his teacher how frustrated he feels with his father gone. Atian says, "Three years in prison for *him* isn't fair to *me*!"

Jermaine talks to his grandpa about the boys on his team.
He always feels better after Grandpa listens.

Lacey tells Mama Jen how much she misses Mommy. And Mama Jen takes Lacey for a visit. Lacey feels fearful going inside tall fences and hearing doors lock behind them.

In this prison, Lacey can hug Mommy twice—at the beginning of the visit and at the end. Mommy sings their special bedtime song. Now Lacey sings it every night.

Not everyone can visit. The jail or prison may be far away, or traveling there may cost too much money. Another way to stay close is by talking on the phone or sending emails or letters.

Xavier's dad calls him on the phone. After they talk, Xavier feels great. He doesn't have to keep secrets from his dad.

Rashid is still too angry to talk on the phone with his mom. Maybe next time she calls he'll be ready.

Rafael mails a picture he drew to his papa. He hopes
Papa will send him a drawing too.

Yen likes writing letters. Her mother wrote back and answered every question:

My Sweet Yen,

I'm here because I broke the law. I will be here until you are twelve years old. It is *not* your fault. I will never stop loving you.

You and I may be
far apart,
but you're always close
to me in my heart.

A Note to Parents, Caregivers, Teachers, and Counselors from the Author

The experiences of the children in *Far Apart, Close in Heart* are very real for more than 2.7 million children in the United States who have a parent in prison or jail. These children need to talk to someone about their feelings, concerns, and questions. Parents and caregivers may wonder what to tell them. Adults can begin by listening, being truthful, accepting and honoring the child's feelings, and helping the child stay connected to the parent.

Often children are confused because they have learned that only bad people go to jail. Keeping in mind that every parent is an important part of a child's sense of self, a caregiver can explain that the issue is not whether the parent is a good or bad person; it is whether they have broken a law. Children may feel encouraged to learn that many adults work for prison reform, criminal justice reform, and ending mass incarceration. And reading *Far Apart, Close in Heart* together can reassure a child that he or she is not the only one going through this situation.

Further Reading:

National Resource Center on Children and Families of the Incarcerated. www.nrccfi.camden.rutgers.edu.

Parenting Inside Out. *How to Talk about Jails and Prisons with Children: A Caregiver's Guide.* www.parentinginsideout.org/wp-content/uploads/2012/09/Talking-About-Jails-and-Prisons2012.pdf.

Prison Policy Initiative. www.prisonpolicy.org.

San Francisco Children of Incarcerated Parents Partnership. *Bill of Rights for Children of Incarcerated Parents.* www.sfcipp.org/images/brochure.pdf.

Sesame Street. *Little Children, Big Challenges: Incarceration.* www.sesamestreet.org/parents/topicsandactivities/toolkits/incarceration.

Youth.gov. www.youth.gov/youth-topics/children-of-incarcerated-parents.

Tips for Adults

When a parent goes to prison or jail, children mourn the loss of the parent who cared for them or the parent they wish had been there. This grief is complicated because the parent didn't die but is mostly out of reach. Children depend on adults in their everyday lives to help them cope and understand their feelings. Caregivers and other adults often struggle to find the words to comfort or explain. They too can be traumatized by the incarceration of the child's parent.

This book is a wonderful tool that adults can use, as it provides an array of situations and not just one or two examples of typical child reactions in the wake of parental incarceration. Start by sharing this story and asking children to choose characters they identify with. The two most important themes to emphasize are that lots of children share the feeling of sadness or confusion or anger and children of incarcerated parents come from many different communities and family situations.

Here are additional strategies that may help:

Talk about feelings with children before you distract them or change the subject. Remember to first reflect on your own feelings, as any bias or judgment can color your reactions. Children need to talk about their feelings to minimize trauma. Remember that young children often express feelings through behavior rather than through words so tantrums, sibling squabbles, tummy aches, and *big* reactions to little upsets are very common for children experiencing the loss of a parent to incarceration. Acknowledge the feeling behind the behavior and seek the help of a health care provider if the behavior persists.

Find developmentally appropriate ways to tell the truth. It is tempting to tell children that parents are away and not say where, or tell them that their parent is at school or in the military or in the hospital. Parents may feel that the child will be less troubled by these explanations. However, research shows that children are less anxious when they know the truth. Children sense there is more than what they are being told and what they imagine is far worse.

If possible, help children visit and communicate with their parent by letter and phone. Be sure to check with the facility about what you can wear on a visit and what can be sent by mail. (For example, many prisons will not allow pictures drawn with markers.)

A common complaint when visiting or calling is that children don't have anything to talk about. Even young children are afraid if they talk about their life it will make their parent sad. Let them know that their mom or dad likes to hear about the day-to-day activities, even when it makes them miss their children.

The hardest questions children have are the ones you can't answer. For example, *when is Dad coming home?* may need a vague answer like, *we think it will be after three birthdays.* Putting exact dates may set everyone up for disappointment when the process takes longer than expected.

Finally, explore options for support groups, summer camps, and other programs that bring children with incarcerated parents together. There is nothing like learning firsthand that you are not alone.

Ann Adalist-Estrin
National Resource Center on Children
and Families of the Incarcerated